MN01152672

AL-KHWARIZMI

FATHER OF ALGEBRA AND TRIGONOMETRY

AL-KHWARIZMI
FATHER OF ALGEBRA AND TRIGONOMETRY

BRIDGET LIM
AND CORONA BREZINA

ROSEN
PUBLISHING®

New York

Published in 2017 by The Rosen Publishing Group, Inc.
29 East 21st Street, New York, NY 10010
Copyright © 2017 by The Rosen Publishing Group, Inc.
First Edition

Library of Congress Cataloging-in-Publication Data
Names: Lim, Bridget | Brezina, Corona.
Title: Al-Khwarizmi : father of algebra and trigonometry / Bridget Lim and
  Corona Brezina.
Description: First edition. | New York : Rosen Publishing, 2017. | Series:
  Physicians, scientists, and mathematicians of the Islamic world |
  Audience: Grades 7-12. | Includes bibliographical references and index.
Identifiers: LCCN 2015047772 | ISBN 9781508171447 (library bound)
Subjects: LCSH: Khuwaarizmai, Muohammad ibn Mausaa, active
813-846--Juvenile literature. | Mathematicians--Iraq--Biography--Juvenile
literature. |
  Muslim mathematicians--Iraq--Biography--Juvenile literature. |
  Astronomers--Iraq--Biography--Juvenile literature. | Mathematics,
  Arab--Juvenile literature. | Astronomy, Arab--Juvenile literature.
Classification: LCC QA29.K44 L56 2017 | DDC 509.2--dc23
LC record available at http://lccn.loc.gov/2015047772

Manufactured in China

CONTENTS

When studying the Middle Ages (about 500 CE–1500 CE) in history class, many of us learn about the period known as the Dark Ages. This was a period during which scientific discovery in Europe came to a grinding halt and there was little emphasis placed on the arts and learning. Few members of the population were educated during these Dark Ages, and little scholarly work was done outside of Catholic monasteries. This focus on Western history leads us to believe that there was almost no intellectual advancement in our world during that vast period of time.

In the Middle East, however, a vast Islamic empire began spreading throughout the region, in addition to North Africa, eventually extending all the way to Spain and India. As the empire grew, its scholars began collecting knowledge from the conquered cultures. This harvesting of intellectual works led to Islam's golden age of cultural and scientific achievement, which lasted from about 750 to 1258. Within the great city of Baghdad, Islamic rulers encouraged scholars to translate scientific and philosophical texts into Arabic. Scientists then used them to support their own research. Baghdad rapidly became one of the most sophisticated cities of the world, and Islamic scholars made important advances

One of the elite scholars in Baghdad's prestigious House of Wisdom, al-Khwarizmi is best remembered for his famous work *Al-Jabr wa al-Muqabala*, the text that defined the branch of mathematics known as algebra.

in mathematics, astronomy, geography, and many other sciences. When Europeans finally emerged from the Dark Ages, the translated texts and scientific progress of Islam's golden age helped fuel Europe's own Renaissance.

One of the most influential figures of Islamic science was the ninth-century astronomer, mathematician, and geographer al-Khwarizmi. Al-Khwarizmi lived in Baghdad during the reign of Caliph al-Mamun, a great supporter of science and the arts. Al-Khwarizmi worked at the House of Wisdom, an academy established by al-Mamun for research and translation of classic texts of antiquity. Scholars at the House of Wisdom studied and translated the works of Greece, Babylonia, and other cultures. Al-Khwarizmi drew on Hindu sources for two of his major works.

Al-Khwarizmi is best remembered for his famous work *Al-Jabr wa al-Muqabala,* the text that defined the branch of mathematics known as algebra. The word "algebra" is derived from the title of al-Khwarizmi's work. Mathematicians of other cultures had developed some basic algebraic concepts, but al-Khwarizmi was the first mathematician to present the elements of algebra in a systematic form.

Al-Khwarizmi's other great mathematical work was his treatise on Hindu numerals. The Arabic system of numbers used today is of Hindu origin. Al-Khwarizmi's treatise explained the decimal place value system and the concept of zero. Centuries after his death, it was translated into Latin and became influential in introducing Hindu numerals to Europe. The Latin translation was titled *Algoritmi de Numero Indorum*, or *Al-Khwarizmi Concerning the Hindu Art of Reckoning.* "Algoritmi" was a Latin transcription of "al-Khwarizmi," but the word gradually changed in spelling and meaning. The modern term "algorithm" is derived from al-Khwarizmi's name.

The scholarship of al-Khwarizmi and other Islamic men of knowledge went on to inspire a renewed interest in learning in Europe. Around the twelfth century, thanks in great part to the work of Islamic scholars, the Italian Renaissance ushered in a revival in classical Greek and Roman culture and spread throughout the continent.

CHAPTER ONE

ISLAM'S GOLDEN AGE

The heart of Islam's golden age was the city of Baghdad, located in present-day Iraq. Because of the city's enviable location on the banks of the Tigris and Euphrates Rivers and the surrounding fertile land, it attracted a great variety of people. Trade caravans loaded with goods passed through the city, bringing wealth and contributing to the city's diversity. People of many different races, religions, and backgrounds lived together in peace.

During the reign of the Abbasid dynasty, scholars flocked to the city, inspired by the caliph's interest in learning and the establishment of the House of Wisdom. Through the work of these scholars, a wealth of knowledge from other cultures was translated and preserved.

THE PROPHET MUHAMMAD

The prophet Muhammad was born in Mecca in present-day Saudi Arabia in 570 CE. Around the year 610, he was visited by a vision of the archangel Gabriel. Gabriel declared him a prophet of God, or Allah, and more visions followed. Encouraged by his wife and uncle, Muhammad began preaching the messages presented to him in these visions, which were later collected in the Quran, the holy text of Islam.

The prophet Muhammad was forced out of Mecca in 622. His flight to Medina is known as the Hegira.

Few of Mecca's residents were willing to believe Muhammad. In 622 he was forced to flee to Medina (also in present-day Saudi Arabia), an important event in Islamic history known as the *Hegira* (flight). There he made many converts and gained consider-able political and religious authority. In the following years Muhammad and his followers conquered Mecca and surrounding areas, making Muhammad the most powerful ruler in Arabia. He granted religious freedom to Christians and Jews as fellow "peoples of the Book" whose religious beliefs had influenced his own. He also preached against social distinctions based on race or social class.

Muhammad died suddenly in 632. After a brief power struggle among his followers, his cousin Abu Bakr became the first caliph, or successor to the Muslim-controlled territory. A chaotic period followed as various factions claiming descent from Muhammad struggled for control. The Umayyad

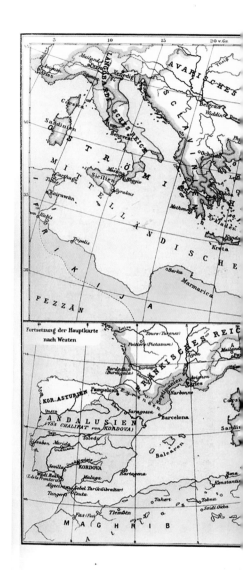

CH DER CHALIFEN UM 750

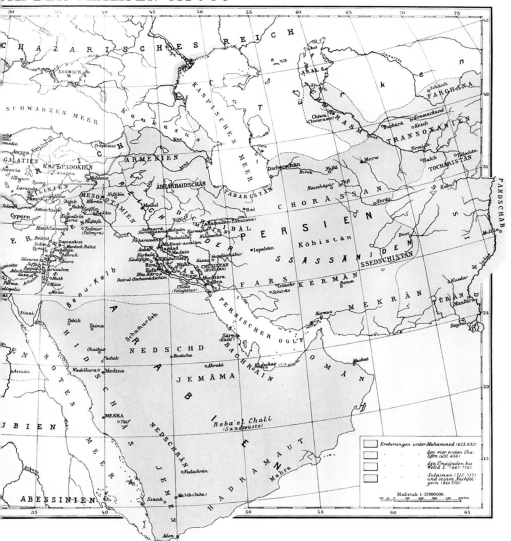

This map shows the Empire of the Caliphate until 750. Pink shading denotes Muhammad's rule from 622–632; orange the first caliphate 632–656; green Caliph al Walid I and the Umayyad Caliphate 661–715; and blue the Caliph Sulaiman/Sulayman bin Abd al-Malik 715–717.

dynasty seized control in 661. At this time, the caliphate's borders included all of the Arabian Peninsula and North Africa. The Umayyads shifted the capital from Medina to Damascus, in present-day Syria, and began expanding their empire. By the early eighth century, the Islamic Empire extended well into central Asia and India. Turkey and Spain were conquered by 715, giving the Umayyads virtually complete control over the Mediterranean Sea.

Following the example set by Muhammad, the caliphs encouraged a degree of religious tolerance. Non-Muslims were allowed to worship as they chose and go about their business in complete freedom as long as they paid a tax and promised not to carry weapons. At first, these freedoms were offered only to Christians and Jews, but as the Islamic Empire conquered parts of India and the remnants of the Persian Empire, these freedoms were also extended to Hindus, Zoroastrians, and other religious sects as well. Nevertheless, non-Muslims were often persecuted by regional officials or blocked from holding government office. Though Muslim rule was a welcome change in regions where religious persecution was common, non-Muslims still found that life became easier once they converted to Islam.

اين كار بى مخاصم و منازع بدست آيد ابو العباس عذر او را قبول كرد و او را

كار او مستقيم شد ابو سلمه را از پيش برداشت و اين قصه در تواريخ بجنبد

Abu al-Abbas al-Saffah became ruler when descendants of Muhammad known as the Abbasids overthrew the Umayyads. The Abbasids made Baghdad their capital. The city would become an important cultural and academic center.

THE CITY OF PEACE

Many Muslims grew discontented with the Umayyad dynasty, as the clan kept political offices in the hands of a few upper-class families from Mecca and Medina and began taxing Muslim lands. Most of the opposition originated in Persia, where many resented the Arab dominance of the region. They rallied behind the Abbasid clan, which claimed descent from Muhammad's uncle Abbas. The Abbasids revolted against the Umayyads in 749, killing the caliph.

The chief of the Abbasid clan, Abu al-Abbas al-Saffah, declared himself caliph in 749. He ruled as Amir al-Muminin, meaning "Commander of the Faithful." The caliph's brother, Abu Jafar al-Mansur began construction of the Abbasid's capital at Baghdad later that year. He chose a spot on the Tigris River not far from the Euphrates River. An extensive system of canals linked the city to a vast network of trade routes and irrigated the surrounding farmland. Trade routes connected the new city to Syria, Persia, Egypt, and beyond. Known as the "City of Peace," Baghdad grew into one of the world's wealthiest and most spectacular cities during the years of Abbasid rule.

Al-Mansur designed Baghdad to serve as the heart of the Muslim world. High walls bristling with towers and a deep moat protected the circular city, while four gates opened in the directions of Syria, the province of Khorasan, and the cities Basra and Kufa. By tradition, the city was also designed to set the caliph apart from the people of the city. An imperial complex, Dar al-Khalifa, formed the city's heart. It was dominated by a large mosque and a magnificent palace. The city's markets and residences all lay outside of the palace.

Under Abbasid rule, Baghdad grew into one of history's great cultural centers. The city and the caliphate experienced one of its richest periods of growth during the reign of Caliph Harun al-Rashid, the fifth caliph of the Abbasid dynasty. A skilled warrior, he led many military campaigns throughout Asia. Harun Al-Rashid expanded the empire as far as the Bosporus Strait and forced the Byzantine capital of Constantinople to pay tribute. As he aged, he turned his attention to diplomacy, maintaining diplomatic ties with China and the European emperor Charlemagne. At home, Baghdad's population soared as people of all races and beliefs flocked to the city. Muslims, Jews, Christians, Zoroastrians, pagans, and others mingled peacefully in Baghdad. However, civil unrest in present-day Syria and Iran brought about by abusive government officials forced Harun al-Rashid to spend a great deal of time living away from the capital.

THE HOUSE OF WISDOM

Harun al-Rashid was a major patron of the arts. Under his rule, Muslim scholars began studying the arts and sciences of other cultures, assimilating Greek and Hindu knowledge into Arabic culture. A poet and scholar himself, he encouraged these arts by inviting a wide range of artists, musicians, and scholars to his palace and treating them with great respect. Many of these artists and scholars came from neighboring countries, bringing new knowledge to Harun al-Rashid's court.

When Harun al-Rashid died in 809, his son Muhammad ibn Harun al-Amin briefly became caliph before his death in 813. Harun al-Rashid's other son, Abu Jafar al-Mamun ibn Harun immediately became the seventh Abbasid caliph. During his reign the caliphate absorbed Afghanistan, the mountains of Persia, and parts of present-day Turkistan. After watching his father deal with numerous revolts throughout his empire, al-Mamun centralized the caliphate's power in Baghdad and limited the influence of regional governors. He also began a program that he called the *mihna*, or inquisition. The mihna was intended to guarantee the loyalty of al-Mamun's subjects and advisers through a series of questions relating to theology, faith, and loyalty. Punishments for failing the tests were harsh, and failure could even result in death.

Despite the harshness of the mihna, al-Mamun's legacy was shaped mostly through his dedication to scholarship. Like Harun al-Rashid, al-Mamun was a scholar and a great patron of artists. He founded an institution for scholars called the *Bayt al-Hikma*, or House of Wisdom. Through the House of Wisdom, al-Mamun encouraged the growth of knowledge in alchemy, mathematics, physics, astronomy, geography, and other fields. The scholars of the House of Wisdom were instrumental in translating scientific texts from various cultures, such as ancient Greece and India, into Arabic and preserving them for future generations.

DECLINE OF THE ABBASID DYNASTY

Baghdad grew and prospered under al-Mamun's rule. Wealth flowed into the city as caravans and barges on the Tigris and Euphrates Rivers continued to transport goods throughout the ever-expanding empire. Craftsmen, traders, and scholars seeking their fortunes flocked to the city. A cultural renaissance inspired by the work of the House of Wisdom was well under

The capital city of Baghdad was situated in a very important location, between the Tigris and Euphrates Rivers. The daily flow of goods from the East to the West ensured that Baghdad attracted traders, scholars, and artisans and also that the city was influenced by a variety of cultures.

way, making Baghdad one of the most scientifically advanced cities of the era.

Al-Mamun left a mixed legacy for his heirs upon his death in 833. The scholastic work carried out by the House of Wisdom and Baghdad's growth brought learning and prosperity to the Islamic Empire. However, the mihna and al-Mamun's attempts to further centralize power only destablized the Islamic Empire, as the subjects stopped trusting the caliphs and began directing their loyalty toward regional officials.

Al-Mamun's half-brother, Abu Ishaq al-Mutasim ibn Harun, ruled as caliph from 833 to 842. During his reign, the caliphate began relying on armies of Turkish slave-soldiers called Mamluks to keep order. In 836, a garrison of mamluks incited a massive riot in Baghdad, forcing al-Mutasim to move the capital to the city of Samarra. Al-Mutasim's son, al-Wathiq ibn Mutasim, succeeded him and ruled until 847. Al-Mutasim and al-Wathiq continued to support the House of Wisdom, which remained in Baghdad. Al-Wathiq himself was an accomplished musician and composed more than one hundred songs.

Al-Wathiq's brother, al-Mutawakkil Ala Allah Jafar bin al-Mutasim, inherited the caliphate. Al-Mutawakkil discontinued the mihna in 848, but he persecuted

واظعته فإن بطل فاخرج منه وردّ ورّ عليه فإن دخل
عليك وطعنك فبطال واحرص أن لا يصل طعنه إليك
ولا تطمع في الطعن وكن حريصا على تبطيل طعنه
وانظر كيف تفعل وهو لا يمكنه أن يأتي بالعقب
بعد ما جرا بينكم ذلك فافهمه

باب الإدمان بالرمح والعمل به

وشوأنتكس بمن دقه عليط من س حبي
نحو الطعن ويكون طول يد الرجل وتعمل فيها

many of the religious minorities living in the Islamic Empire. Minority sects within Islam were repressed, as were Christians, Jews, and other minorities.

Al-Mutawakkil was less interested in learning or art than his brother and his father, and the House of Wisdom declined rapidly during his rule. He did, however, have a keen eye for beauty and an interest in buildings. During his lifetime, his builders completed at least twenty new palaces and the Great Mosque of Samarra, known for its spiral minaret.

Al-Mutawakkil was assassinated in 861, after which the Abbasid dynasty declined rapidly. Rebelling regional governors began splitting away from the Islamic Empire, making use of dissatisfied Mamluk forces to drive their rebellions. The capital was restored to Baghdad in 892, a move meant to symbolize the return of Abbasid dominance, but the city had also declined. Mongol forces put an end to Abbasid power in 1258 by looting Baghdad and killing the caliph and hundreds of thousands of people, an attack from which the great city never fully recovered.

AN EMPHASIS ON LEARNING

The Islamic Empire was vast in both geographical scale and in cultural diversity. Many different cultures and traditions were allowed to survive within its boundaries under the rule of the caliphs. The caliphate's encouragement of learning contributed to the translation and preservation of a great deal of knowledge from these various cultures.

Upon the foundation of the Islamic Empire, the earliest conquests made by Muhammad and his followers were of the regions surrounding the valleys of the Nile, the Tigris, and the Euphrates Rivers. These areas had been settled for thousands of years and were home to advanced cultures. Some of these regions, particularly in Egypt, had been occupied by the Roman Empire before its collapse. During the years of Roman rule, scholars in Egypt studied the science and philosophy of the ancient Greeks. The conquering Arabs were a literate people, and they were extremely impressed by the information they gained through the Egyptians. The ruling caliphs of the Islamic Empire, particularly members of the Abbasid dynasty in Baghdad, actively sought to expand their knowledge and began encouraging scholars from other parts of the world to join their courts.

A CLASSIC TALE

Shortly before the middle of the tenth century, a Baghdad scholar named al-Jahshiyari compiled tales for what would later become the classic *A Thousand and One Nights* (*Alf Laylah wa-Laylah*). In the story, the queen Scheherazade is condemned to die by her husband, the sultan Schahriar. The night before her execution, she tells a story to her sister so that the sultan will overhear. She stops before she finishes the tale, and the curious sultan allows her to live another day so that she can tell the rest the next night. Scheherazade repeats this pattern for a thousand and one nights, until the sultan relents and removes the death sentence.

Al-Jahshiyari based his work on an old Persian text called *A Thousand Tales* (*Hazar Afsana*), which consisted of stories originating in ancient India. *Hazar Afsana* provided the work's structure and many of the character names, including Scheherazade. He incorporated anecdotes and folk tales from the oral folk traditions of Persia, Egypt, and Arabia. Historical figures were also added to the work. In particular, the court of Caliph Harun al-Rashid was used as the setting for many humorous escapades and romances. Other writers continued adding tales to *A Thousand and One Nights* until it reached its present form in the late fifteenth century. Today it remains widely popular due to its exotic background and the appeal of characters like Ali Baba, Aladdin, and Sinbad the Sailor, which were added later.

In the Islamic tradition, scholarship and knowledge were spread through a system of religious and legal schools called *madrasas*. Often associated with local mosques, these schools focused on religious and philosophical instruction throughout the Islamic Empire. Students of the madrasas learned to read, write, and do basic mathematics. Most of their instruction centered around the Quran, the book revealed to Muhammad. Instructors within the madrasas taught their students how to interpret the Quran's words, according to the interpretation of the instructors. Accomplished students of the madrasas often made their way to Baghdad, where some found places within the House of Wisdom established by Caliph al-Mamun.

One of the primary goals of the House of Wisdom was the translation of classic texts from all over the known world into Arabic. Many of the manuscripts came from ancient Greece, while others arrived from India. The translations were stored in the library of the House of Wisdom along with records of the scientific discoveries made by Islamic scientists. All of these translations, documents, and records were easily accessible to other scholars.

In 751, paper manufactured from rags or tree bark was introduced to the Islamic Empire from China.

Madrasas were learning institutions that focused on religious and legal education. Students learned the fundamentals, including how to read the Quran.

Earlier forms of writing material, such as papyrus made from woven reeds or vellum made from calf skin, were costly to produce and purchase. By 793, a facility had been built in Baghdad for manufacturing paper. Scholars were thankful to have access to an inexpensive writing material, which helped them increase their written output.

The vast number of texts translated and preserved by the House of Wisdom allowed Islamic scholars and scientists access to information gathered in distant places and time periods. They could then combine and expand on these ideas in their own texts, making new discoveries as they progressed in their studies. Their translations and new discoveries also spread throughout the Islamic Empire, ending up in provincial libraries and schools through the empire's vast trade network. Many of the works that survived the end of the Abbasid dynasty later helped to reawaken Europe's interest in learning. Translated from Arabic into Latin or Greek, they formed the basis for the European Renaissance and the core of Europe's scientific, philosophical, and literary growth.

HIS LIFE AS WE KNOW IT

. . . .

As with most of the great Islamic thinkers of the golden age, very little is known about al-Khwarizmi's life. Most biographical details come from bibliographical entries made by scholars at the time and brief references by Islamic historians and geographers. Some of these sources are open to interpretation, and other remarks are of questionable accuracy. Most historical records focus on al-Khwarizmi's scholarly work. They allude to his writings and his accomplishments as a mathematician, astronomer, and geographer. Historians make almost no mention of his personal life.

We can surmise that Abu Jafar Muhammad ibn Musa al-Khwarizmi came from Khwarizm, or Khorezm, a region in central Asia south of the Aral Sea. Khwarizm was a once a thriving kingdom of antiquity. It later became a province of the Persian Empire, and the region fell under control of the Islamic rulers in 680. Today, Khwarizm is the city of Khiva in Uzbekistan.

Al-Khwarizmi's name is sometimes transcribed in English as al-Khowarizmi, al-Khawarizmi, and al-Khwarizimi.

The historian G. J. Toomer hypothesizes in *The Dictionary of Scientific Biography*, however, that it was actually al-Khwarizmi's family that originally came from Khwarizm, not al-Khwarizmi himself. Other historians dispute his theory. Uzbekistan proudly counts al-Khwarizmi as one of the nation's great historical figures.

The exact year of al-Khwarizmi's birth is also not known. He was probably born around 780, shortly before Harun al-Rashid became caliph.

AL-MAMUN: PATRON OF SCIENCE AND LEARNING

Al-Khwarizmi was appointed a member of the House of Wisdom by the caliph al-Mamun, who reigned from 813 to 833. He dedicated two of his early works,

The Banu Musa brothers published *The Book of Ingenious Devices* in 850. Al-Khwarizmi was at the House of Wisdom at the same time as the Banu Musa brothers.

Al-Jabr wa al-Muqabala and *Zij*, which is a treatise on astronomy, to the caliph. Al-Mamun was succeeded by his brother al-Mutasim (reigned 833–842) and later al-Mutasim's elder son al-Wathiq (r. 842–847). The Abbasid dynasty declined under al-Wathiq's brother al-Mutawakkil, who reigned from 847 to 861. Al-Khwarizmi served under all of these caliphs, though al-Mamun is best remembered as a patron of science and learning. In the introduction to his work on algebra, al-Khwarizmi extravagantly thanks and praises al-Mamun.

> That fondness for science, by which God has distinguished the IMAN AL MAMUN, the Commander of the Faithful (besides the caliphate which He has vouchsafed unto him by lawful succession, in the robe of which He has invested him, and with the honors of which He has adorned him), that affability and condescension which he shows to the learned, that promptitude with which he protects and supports them in the elucidation of obscurities and in the removal of difficulties—has encouraged me to compose a short work.

There is no evidence that al-Khwarizmi's loyalty to the caliphs ever wavered.

Al-Khwarizmi is considered by many to have been the greatest scholar of his day. In his book *Introduction to the History of Science*, the historian George Sarton refers to the first half of the ninth century as "the time of al-Khwarizmi." (According to Sarton, the second half of the eighth century was "the time of Jabar ibn Haiyan," an alchemist, and the second half of the ninth century was "the time of al-Razi," who is best remembered as a physician.) Baghdad during this period was one of the great intellectual centers of the world, however, and many of al-Khwarizmi's colleagues in the House of Wisdom are known for significant contributions to science and philosophy.

One of al-Khwarizmi's contemporaries at the House of Wisdom, Abu Yusuf Yaqub ibn Ishaq ibn al-Kindi (circa 801–873), is known as the first great Muslim philosopher. Al-Kindi translated many works of Aristotle into Arabic, and his own philosophy was heavily influenced by Aristotle's writings and Neoplatonism, a reinterpretation of Plato. He contended in his philosophical works that the conclusions of religion and philosophy could be reconciled but that philosophy and reason were inferior to the divine insight of religion. His works deal with a variety of subjects and include an important treatise on optics, the first known Muslim discussion of music, and writings on medicine and physics. Like al-Khwarizmi, al-Kindi was also a

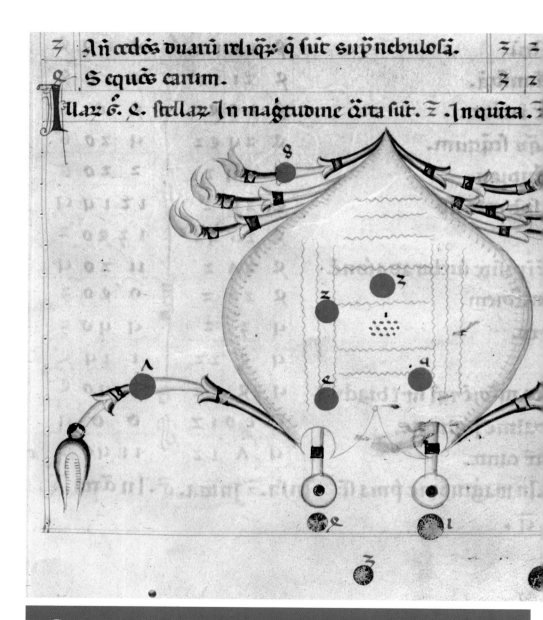

The great minds at the House of Wisdom made many advances in astronomy. Al-Mamun set up unrivaled observatories. It is believed that al-Khwarizmi participated in experiments to determine the size of Earth, using the terrestrial degree.

mathematician and astronomer. Al-Kindi was persecuted late in his career by Caliph al-Mutawakkil, who maintained a strictly orthodox interpretation of Islam.

Al-Khwarizmi also worked at the House of Wisdom at the same time as the three Banu Musa brothers, Jafar Muhammad, al-Hasan, and Ahmad. *Banu Musa* means "the sons of Musa." Their father, Musa ibn Shakir, was a former robber who became an able astrologer later in his life. The brothers are best remembered for their work in geometry, but Ahmad was also interested in mechanics. In *Kitab al-Hiyal, or The Book of Ingenious Devices*, he describes a contraption that would deliver hot and cold water, devices for digging wells, and a lamp with a self-trimming wick. Along with al-Khwarizmi, the Banu Musa brothers were the leading researchers of the House of Wisdom. They also supervised the translators working at the House of Wisdom and led astronomical observations.

During al-Mamun's reign, astronomers at the House of Wisdom undertook the operation of measuring a terrestrial degree. A terrestrial degree is the length on land of one degree of arc in the sky. With this information, they could determine the size of Earth. They computed the length of a terrestrial degree to be 56 2/3 Arabic miles, a distance we now know to be in error by about 2,877 feet (877 meters). According to this figure, Earth would be about 20,400 miles (32,831 kilometers) in circumference and 6,500 miles (10,461 km) in diameter. In reality, Earth has a circumference of 24,902 miles (40,076 km) and a diameter of 7,900 miles (12,714 km) at the equator. The Banu Musa brothers and al-Khwarizmi almost certainly participated in the project.

AL-KHWARIZMI'S RELIGION

After becoming a member of the House of Wisdom, al-Khwarizmi lived and worked in Baghdad for the rest of his life. Historical records leave almost no clues about his daily activities, travel, family and friends, or reaction to the reception of his work. Historians have speculated on al-Khwarizmi's native language. Since he was born in a former Persian province, he may have spoken the Persian language. It is also possible that he spoke Khwarezmian, a language of the region that is now extinct. Although the caliph's court welcomed non-Islamic scientists, they had a lower status than Muslims. Nonbelievers were not free to openly express ideas contrary to orthodox Islam. In his book *The Universal History of Numbers*, the scholar George Ifrah quotes al-Biruni, a native of Khwarizm, on the Islamic repression of Khwarizm's culture.

> Thus Qutaybah did away with those who knew the script of Khwarizm, who understood the country's traditions and taught the knowledge of its inhabitants; he submitted them to tortures so that they were wrapped up in shadows and no one could know (even in Khwarizm) what had (preceded) or followed the birth of Islam.

Qutaybah ibn-Muslim was the governor of the province of Khorasan and a conqueror who greatly expanded the Islamic Empire to the west during the early eighth century.

Al-Biruni's testimony brings up the question of al-Khwarizmi's religion. The historian al-Tabari referred to al-Khwarizmi in one instance as "al-Majusi" in his *Tarikh ur-Rusul wal-Muluk* (*History of the Prophets and Kings*, often referred to simply as his *Annals*). This seems to indicate that he practiced the Zoroastrian religion. Al-Khwarizmi reveals very little personal information in his writings. He did, however, offer thanks to God in the introduction to his work on algebra.

> Prais'd be God for his bounty towards those who deserve it by their virtuous acts … He sent MOHAMMED (on whom may the blessing of God repose!) with the mission of a prophet, long after any messenger from above had appeared, when justice had fallen into neglect, and when the true way of life was sought for in vain. Through him he was cured of blindness, and saved through him from perdition, and increased through him what before was small, and collected through him what before was scattered. Praised be God our Lord! and may his glory increase, and may all his names be hallowed — besides whom there is no God; and may his benediction rest on MOHAMMED the Prophet and on his descendants!

Al-Khwarizmi's words make it clear that he was an orthodox Muslim. It is possible that al-Tabari meant that al-Khwarizmi's family was once Zoroastrian or that al-Khwarizmi was Zoroastrian when he was younger. If

This fifteenth-century illustration shows Zoroaster and two demons. Zoroastrianism was founded by the prophet Zoroaster in the second millennium BCE. It dominated the Iranian empires until it was replaced by Islam.

THE ANCIENT RELIGION ZOROASTRIANISM

Al-Khwarizmi was not a Zoroastrian himself, but this ancient religion was still widely practiced during the years of the Abbasid dynasty. Zoroastrianism is a religion named for its founder, the prophet Zoroaster, who likely lived in ancient Persia during the seventh century BCE. Virtually nothing is known about his life, but he established the core teachings of his faith in a collection of psalms called the Gathas. Zoroastrianism is based on the worship of Ahura Mazda, the Lord Wisdom. All of the good in the universe comes from Ahura Mazda's creative force, called Spenta Mainyu. Spenta Mainyu is assisted by six entities: Good Mind, Truth, Health, Life, Power, and Devotion. Spenta Mainyu's twin and opposite, Angra Mainyu, is the source of all evil. Whereas Spenta Mainyu represents truth, Angra Mainyu represents lies, or falseness. Upon death, people who follow truth and the way of Spenta Mainyu will cross over to paradise, while followers of lies and Angra Mainyu are sent to a fiery underworld.

Zoroastrianism eventually spread throughout Asia, but Persia remained the religion's stronghold for many centuries. Many of the emperors of ancient Persia were Zoroastrians, starting with Darius I, who ruled from 521–486 BCE. When the Sassanid dynasty took the Persian throne in 224 CE, it made Zoroastrianism Persia's state religion. The Islamic Empire's conquest of Persia in the seventh century ended Zoroastrian dominance, and the sect declined as the region's population converted to Islam. Today, there are an estimated 250,000 Zoroastrians worldwide, most of whom live around Bombay, India.

he did convert to Islam from Zoroastrianism, the move would have greatly benefited his position at court.

A POSSIBLE MEETING WITH THE KHAZARS

Historical records show that in 842, Caliph al-Wathiq may have sent al-Khwarizmi to the northern Caucasus mountain region to meet with the chief of the Khazars. The Khazars were an ancient people who controlled trade between the Caspian Sea and the Black Sea. It is possible, however, that it was Mohammad the Banu Musa brother who traveled to the Caucasus, not al-Khwarizmi. Similarly, it was probably Mohammad the Banu Musa brother who made an expedition to Greece to investigate the tomb of the Seven Sleepers of Ephesus.

According to legend, the Sleepers were seven Christian youths who took refuge in a cave from the religious persecution of the Roman emperor Decius. The emperor had the cave boarded up, but the Seven Sleepers woke from a sleep two hundred years later. Their existence reaffirmed the faith of Emperor Theodosius II, and they returned to sleep in the cave until the Day of Judgment. The legend, thought to be

The Seven Sleepers fled Ephesus because of their religious beliefs and hid in a cave. They awoke many years later to find the world had changed drastically.

of Syrian origin, was popular among both Muslims and Christians. An Islamic version of the tale is known as "Surat al-Kahf," or "The Men of the Cave." The historian and scientist al-Biruni wrote that in the ninth century, corpses of monks believed to have been the Seven Sleepers were displayed in a cave. Even though al-Khwarizmi may not have himself traveled to the Caucasus or to Greece, these accounts give an idea of some of the more exceptional duties of the scholars of the House of Wisdom.

The last known historical reference to al-Khwarizmi is in al-Tabari's *Annals*. A group of astronomers attended to Caliph al-Wathiq as he lay on his death-bed in 847. They consulted the stars and assured him that he would reign for fifty more years. Nonetheless, the caliph died ten days later. If al-Tabari was correct in naming al-Khwarizmi as one of the astronomers present, he would have been nearly seventy years old. Most sources list "about 850" as the year of his death.

THE SCHOLARSHIP OF AL-KHWARIZMI'S

Al-Khwarizmi wrote a number of groundbreaking works during his long career.

His most famous work, of course, is his *Al-Jabr wa al-Muqabala*, which laid the foundations for modern algebra. He completed both this work and *Zij*, his astronomical treatise, during al-Mamun's reign from 813 to 833.

Of his other works, only *Istikhraj Ta'rikh al-Yahud*, *About the Jewish Calendar*, a short work on the Jewish calendar, can be dated. Calculations within the text mention that al-Khwarizmi worked on it during 823 and

824. His work on Hindu numerals, the basis for the Arabic system of numbers we use today, was composed sometime after *Al-Jabr wa al-Muqabala*. He wrote *Kitab al-tar'ikh*, or *Chronicle*, a history account based on astrology, sometime after 826. His other major work was his *Geography—Kitab Surat al-Ard*, or *Book of the Form of the Earth*.

Al-Khwarizmi's residency at the House of Wisdom yielded an impressive body of work, although little has survived until today.

Al-Khwarizmi wrote his works in Arabic. During the

golden age of Islam, Arabic was nearly the universal language of the intellectual world. As Islamic scientists absorbed knowledge from other cultures, the Arabic language had to incorporate new concepts. The Arabic vocabulary expanded, and existing words were adapted to new needs. The Arabic language became the best language of the time for expressing scientific thought.

Only a few of al-Khwarizmi's works have been preserved in their original Arabic. A couple exist in Latin translations. Some have been lost and are known only because of references in other sources from the time.

Al-Khwarizmi is primarily remembered today as a mathematician, but he was also an outstanding astronomer and geographer. It was quite common for scholars of his day to explore many fields of study. In addition, different areas of expertise were not as sharply differentiated as they are today. Most mathematicians, for example, also studied astronomy or astrology. Al-Khwarizmi's colleagues al-Kindi and the Banu Musa brothers explored a variety of subjects. Al-Farabi (ca. 870–ca. 950), for example, was an important philosopher, but he also studied mathematics, music, and medicine. The great scholar al-Biruni (973–1048) was a historian, mathematician, scientist, philosopher, and traveler.

One of the most famous figures of medieval Islam, Omar Khayyam (1048–1123), was a mathematician and astronomer as well as the author of the *Rubayyat*, which means "quatrains." In one of the verses (translated by Edward Fitzgerald), Khayyam playfully refers to his work in reforming the Persian calendar.

> Ah, but my Computations, People say,
> Reduced the Year to better reckoning?—Nay
> 'Twas only striking from the Calendar
> Unborn To-morrow, and dead Yesterday.

As a mathematician who studied algebra, Khayyam was undoubtedly quite familiar with al-Khwarizmi's work. In addition, both men studied and wrote about calendars.

AL-KHWARIZMI'S MATHEMATICAL SCHOLARSHIP

Under the patronage of the caliphs, scientists and philosophers of the medieval Islamic world studied and built upon the scholarship—including mathematical knowledge—of ancient civilizations. Al-Khwarizmi and other scholars at the House of Wisdom translated and studied mathematical manuscripts inherited from cultures of antiquity, especially the classic texts of ancient Greece. Mathematicians from Persia, Damascus, India, and other regions of the Islamic Empire were invited to Baghdad and other centers of learning and culture. New trade routes also opened exchanges of information from one culture to another. The Muslim caliphs were great conquerors as well, and as they seized new territory, they also seized the closely guarded secrets of other cultures.

Islamic mathematicians assimilated and systemized the mathematical scholarship of these various sources.

This painting depicts a Christian and a Muslim practicing geometry together. At the House of Wisdom, as well as other revered Muslim learning institutions, scholars studied the works of ancient Greek philsophers and scientists and then built upon them using their Islamic point of view.

In turn, they contributed greatly to the development of mathematics, especially to the branches of arithmetic, algebra, geometry, and trigonometry.

ANCIENT MATHEMATICS

In his book *The Universal History of Numbers*, Georges Ifrah points out that most human societies have developed some method of numerical notation and that even some animals have an innate "sense of number." The Egyptians and Babylonians were the first cultures to develop an organized system of mathematics.

The earliest existing Egyptian mathematical papyruses date from about 1750 BCE. The Egyptians used a decimal system of numbering, meaning that numbers are expressed in powers of ten. Specific hieroglyphics represented 1, 100, 1,000, 10,000, 100,000, and 1,000,000. The Egyptians also had a simplistic system for calculating fractions. Their mathematical processes involved little more than arithmetic and basic geometry necessary for calculations in agriculture, trade, and the construction of monuments such as the pyramids.

The Babylonians of Mesopotamia developed a more advanced system of mathematics as early as 1950 BCE. Ancient cuneiform tablets show that they

Early cultures developed their own numbering systems. This fourteenth-century manuscript page is taken from *Treatise on the Question of Arithmetic Code* by the Master Ala-El-Din Muhammed El Ferjumedhi.

used a sexagesimal system of numbering—it was based on the number 60 rather than 10. Today, measurement of time is based on a sexagesimal system. There are sixty seconds in a minute and sixty minutes in an hour.

The Babylonians made a significant mathematical achievement in establishing a place value system in their numbering. Today, our decimal system of numbers uses a place system with a ones place, a tens place, a hundreds place, and so on. The Babylonians had fifty-nine different roughly wedge-shaped numbers. The number 60 was represented by the same symbol as the number 1, but it was moved over one place value. Babylonian mathematicians made advances in arithmetic, including long division and multiplication, fractions, and geometry. They were also familiar with some basic algebraic concepts.

It was the Greeks who transformed mathematics from a practical calculating tool into a logical system. The Greeks drew on Egyptian and Babylonian knowledge, but they established abstract definitions, laws, and proofs for mathematical concepts. One of the first great Greek mathematicians was Pythagoras of Samos, who lived during the sixth century BCE. He believed that everything in the world could be understood

Pythagoras and Euclid meet in this fifteenth-century marble tile. The Greeks took mathematics beyond the practical.

through mathematics. He even believed there were numbers for such concepts as justice and the soul.

The most famous Greek mathematician was Euclid, who taught at the famous school of Alexandria during the third century BCE. He compiled Greek knowledge of geometry into a thirteen-volume work called the *Elements*. It is famous for its logic and clarity, and translations were used as a text in schools until the nineteenth century. After Euclid, mathematicians such as Archimedes, Apollonius of Perga, and Claudius Ptolemy made further advances in geometry.

The Greeks used what is called an acrophonic system of numbers. Numbers were represented by the first letter of the Greek name for the number. The notation was very similar to the Egyptian hieroglyphic system.

Islamic scholars translated the texts of Aristotle, Euclid, Archimedes, Ptolemy, Apollonius, and other Greek mathematicians, as well as works from China, India, and ancient Babylonia. Persian, Sanskrit, Koptic, and Aramaic knowledge was also translated and preserved. Islamic mathematicians wrote commentaries on these ancient and foreign texts, refined and expanded their mathematical knowledge, and built on each other's work. Copies of translations and original works by Islamic scholars were circulated to universities and libraries across the empire. After the decline of the Islamic state, many of these manuscripts survived, especially in Spanish institutions.

Al-Khwarizmi represents both facets of Muslim scholarship. He made original contributions to mathematics and also worked to preserve and transmit mathematical knowledge from other cultures. His most famous work, the *Al-Jabr wa al-Muqabala*, opened up a whole new discipline of mathematics. Al-Khwarizmi also wrote a treatise that introduced and explained Hindu numerals and methods of calculations.

These pages of an Arabic manuscript copy of al-Khwarizmi's *Al-Jabr wa al-Muqabala* show solutions to quadratic equations. The book was written to solve practical problems that Muslims might encounter in the course of their daily lives. Al-Khwarizmi defines algebra as a separate discipline in these pages.

THE CONTENTS OF *AL-JABR WA AL-MUQABALA*

Modern algebra is the branch of mathematics in which numbers and other elements of equations can be represented by letters. Algebra provides a generalization of arithmetic. The equation $a + a = 2a$, for example, will be true for any number that the letter a might represent. Algebraic math problems often require that the student solve an equation by finding the value for an unknown variable, often x. In the equation $ax^2 + bx = c$, for example, a, b, and c are replaced with numbers. The value of x will depend on the value of a, b, and c, but the equation can always be solved by using the same mathematical processes.

Al-Khwarizmi did not set out to found a new branch of mathematics when he wrote *Al-Jabr wa al-Muqabala*. In the introduction to the work, he declares his intent in very practical terms. He describes his text in this way:

> A short work on Calculating by (the rules of) Completion and Reduction confining it to what is easiest and most useful in arithmetic, such as men constantly require in cases of inheritance, legacies, partition, law-suits, and trade, and in all their dealings with one another, or where the measuring of lands, the

digging of canals, geometrical computation, and other objects of various sorts and kinds are concerned.

Al-Khwarizmi wanted his work to help people solve mathematical dilemmas in their everyday lives.

The full title is *Kitab al-Jabr wa al-Muqabala*, although the *Kitab*, which merely means "book," is rarely used when referring to the work. *Al-Jabr* refers to the removal of negative terms from a mathematical equation. *Muqabala* means reduction or balancing the equation to a simpler form. *Al-Jabr wa al-Muqabala* as a whole has come to mean generally "the process of performing algebraic operations."

The book consists of three sections. The first part is the theoretical basis of what we now know as algebra. The second is concerned with mensuration, or the geometry of computing lengths, areas, and volumes. The final section is on legacies, and it deals with the mathematics of Islamic inheritance laws.

The first part begins by introducing the reader to numbers.

When I consider what people generally want in calculating, I found that it always is a number. I also observed that every number is composed of units, and that any number may be divided into units.

Moreover, I found that every number which may be expressed from one to ten, surpasses the preceding by one unit: afterwards the ten is doubled or tripled just as before the units were: thus arise twenty, thirty, etc. until a hundred: then the hundred is doubled and tripled in the same manner as the units and the tens, up to a thousand . . . so forth to the utmost limit of numeration.

Al-Khwarizmi uses no symbols or written equations throughout his work. Every mathematical process is expressed in words.

After introducing numbers, al-Khwarizmi moves on to the process of solving mathematical equations. He discusses both linear and quadratic equations, two types of basic algebraic equations. According to al-Khwarizmi, all linear and quadratic equations can be reduced to six forms:

(1) $ax^2 = bx$

(2) $ax^2 = b$

(3) $ax = b$

(4) $ax^2 + bx = c$

(5) $ax^2 + c = bx$

(6) $ax^2 = bx + c$

The quantities a, b, and c represent known numbers, and x is the unknown quantity. By using numbers in place of a, b, and c, the reader can use al-Khwarizmi's equations to find the numerical value for x.

These six equations are written in modern mathematical notation. Al-Khwarizmi describes the equations in words. For example, he states one problem in these terms:

> A quantity: I multiplied a third of it and a dirham by a fourth of it and a dirham; it becomes twenty.

In modern notation, it is written $(x/3 + 1)(x/4 + 1) = 20$. A dirham is a type of coin, and al-Khwarizmi used it to signify a single numerical unit. He goes on to reduce and solve the equation. Here is the first step of the process:

> Its computation is that you multiply a third of something by a fourth of something: it comes to a half of a sixth of a square. And you multiply a dirham by a third of something: it comes to a third of something; and [you multiply] a dirham by a fourth of something to get a fourth of something; and [you multiply] a dirham by a dirham to get a dirham . . . Thus its total, [namely] a half of a sixth of a square and third of something and a quarter of something and a dirham, is equal to twenty dirhams.

In modern notation, the equation he describes is $x^2/12 + x/3 + x/4 + 1 = 20$. Multiplying out mathematical expressions in this way is a basic process taught today in introductory algebra. Al-Khwarizmi goes on to further simplify the equation and solve for x.

One of al-Khwarizmi's great accomplishments in writing his *Al-Jabr wa al-Muqabala* was the establishment of algebra as a separate branch of mathematics from geometry. Geometry had been known for millennia, and it was thoroughly refined by the Greeks. By contrast, many of al-Khwarizmi's algebraic concepts were original and new to the study of mathematics. Nevertheless, al-Khwarizmi did use geometrical proofs for the answers to some of his equations.

In one case, al-Khwarizmi poses this question to his readers:

> For instance, "one square, and ten roots of the same, amount to thirty-nine dirhams" that is to say, what must be the square which, when increased by ten of its own roots, amount to thirty-nine?

This can be put into modern notation: $x^2 + 10x = 39$. This is an example of a quadratic equation that follows the fourth form of his six types of equations. He then presents the solution:

You halve the number of the roots, which in the present instance yields five. This you multiply by itself; the product is twenty-five. Add this to thirty-nine; the sum is sixty-four.

The equations for these steps are $(x + 5)^2 = 39 + 25 = 64$.

Now take the root of this, which is eight, and subtract from it half the number of the roots, which is five; the remainder is three. This is the root of the square which you sought for; the square itself is nine.

Therefore, $x + 5 = \sqrt{64}$, and $x + 5 = 8$; $x = 3$. Later in the section, al-Khwarizmi demonstrates the solution geometrically by describing a square, "the figure A B, each side of which may be considered as one of its roots." He shows how his algebraic solution can be proved by adding a narrow rectangle to each side of the square and then adding small squares at each corner. The algebraic process demonstrated by this proof is known as "completing the square."

Al-Khwarizmi ends the first part of his *Al-Jabr wa al-Muqabala* with a short section titled "On Business Transactions." It deals with computing quantities, prices, and other practical transactions.

The second section of the work is on mensuration and describes how to compute areas and volumes of various shapes and solids. Al-Khwarizmi gives equations for finding the area and circumference of a circle, for example, and for computing the volumes of cones, pyramids, and truncated pyramids. At one point, he gives a fairly accurate estimate of the number π (pi). Al-Khwarizmi also presents the famous Pythagorean theorem established by the Greeks: $a^2 + b^2 = c^2$. The theorem states that for a right triangle (a triangle with one right angle), the square of the hypoteneuse c (the long side) is equal to the sum of the squares of the two short sides a and b. Al-Khwarizmi's proof of the theorem is different from the proof presented in Euclid's *Elements*, however. This indicates that even if al-Khwarizmi was familiar with the *Elements*, it was not one of his main sources for background research on *Al-Jabr wa al-Muqabala*.

The third and longest part deals with the mathematics of legacies. It consists of problems and solutions involving inheritance according to Islamic laws. The mathematics in this section are fairly simple, but the problems require expertise on the complex Islamic system of inheritance. Under this system, people inherited fixed ratios of the deceased's property based on their relationship with the deceased.

AL-KHWARIZMI'S HINDU NUMERALS

Al-Khwarizmi's treatise on Hindu numerals has been lost. Historians are not even completely sure of the exact title. It is often referred to as *Kitab al Jami' wa'l Tafriq bi-Hisab al-Hind*, or *Indian Technique of Addition and Subtraction*, but it could also have been something like *Kitab Hisab al-Adad al-Hindi*, or *Treatise on Calculation with the Hindu Numerals*. Both possible versions of the title convey al-Khwarizmi's intent in writing this work. It was his introduction of Hindu numbers and methods of calculation to the Islamic intellectual world.

Historians have long debated the precise origin of the Arabic numerals that we use today. It is true that Islamic texts introduced these numerals to the Western world, but they were not invented by Islamic mathematicians. In his book *The Universal History of Numbers*, Georges Ifrah gives convincing evidence that the system of numbers we use today originated in India centuries before the rise of the Islamic Empire. He references the scholar al-Biruni as one of his sources. Al-Biruni lived in India for many years and wrote about Indian mathematics and science in many of his books.

The Indians developed the numbers 1 to 9 and 0, and they established the decimal place value system. Some historians have theorized that their place value system may have been influenced by the Babylonian sexagesimal place value system. One fundamental breakthrough in Indian mathematics was their use of zero as a placeholder. The modern number 50, for

Evolution of Hindu-Arabic numerals

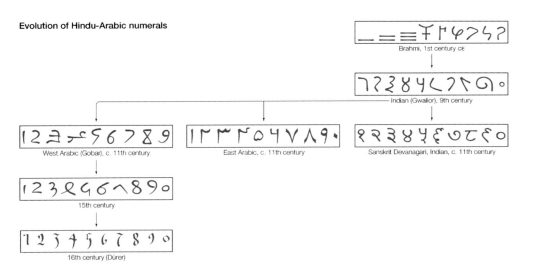

Brahmi, 1st century CE

Indian (Gwalior), 9th century

West Arabic (Gobar), c. 11th century

East Arabic, c. 11th century

Sanskrit Devanagari, Indian, c. 11th century

15th century

16th century (Dürer)

example, contains a five in the tens place and a zero in the ones place. The zero is the placeholder that merely indicates the absence of a number that has an actual value. Most ancient cultures, including the Babylonians and Greeks, did not see the value of having a number that would signify nothing. Today, we are so familiar with using the number zero that we cannot comprehend what a strange concept it would have seemed to scholars first studying the Hindu system of numbers.

Al-Khwarizmi describes the Hindu numerals and the place value system in his treatise. A Latin translation of the work, as quoted by Ifrah, begins by stating al-Khwarizmi's purpose: "We have decided to explain Indian calculating techniques using the nine characters and to show how, because of their simplicity and conciseness, these characters are capable of expressing any number." Al-Khwarizmi does not neglect the zero, "the tenth figure in the shape of a circle" used "so as not to confuse the positions." He also outlines basic addition, subtraction, multiplication, division, and a few other mathematical functions using the Hindu system.

Islamic scholars and scribes were slow to adopt Hindu numerals. Many were unwilling to give up their traditional methods of writing and calculating amounts.

It took even longer for the system to be introduced to Europe.

Al-Khwarizmi's treatise was translated into Latin during the twelfth century. The Latin version, however, is known to be significantly different from al-Khwarizmi's original. It was titled *Algoritmi de Numero Indorum*, or *Al-Khwarizmi Concerning the Hindu Art of Reckoning*. In Latin, al-Khwarizmi's name was first transcribed as *Alchoarismi*, and it gradually evolved into *Algorismi*, *Algorismus*, *Algorisme*, and finally *Algorism* and *Algorithm*. Scholars of late medieval Europe used the term *algorism* in reference to mathematical operations using the new Arabic system of numbers and system of calculation. Today, "algorithm" is a general term for the procedure of solving a mathematical problem, usually by using a precise series of steps. Algorithms in computer programs instruct the computer as to which steps to perform and in what sequence in order to complete a task.

AL-KHWARIZMI THE ASTRONOMER

Al-Khwarizmi's contributions to knowledge don't stop at mathematics. He also was accomplished in the fields of astronomy and geography. Al-Khwarizmi lived during an exciting period in Islamic astronomy. The scholars at the House of Wisdom worked in the famous observatory built by Caliph al-Mamun around 829. Al-Mamun's new observatory attracted scholars and students of astronomy from across the Islamic Empire. Astronomers observed the movements of celestial bodies and improved the astronomical instruments used for observations.

At the same time, scholars translated works on astronomy that contained the knowledge of the Greeks, Babylonians, Egyptians, Indians, and Sassanians. (The Sassanid dynasty of Persia encouraged astronomical research between the third and seventh centuries.) Islamic astronomers built on this knowledge and applied it to both academic and practical purposes. Astronomical observations and calculations were used for calendars, timekeeping, horoscopes, and determination of precise latitudes and longitudes for locations.

THE STUDY OF ASTRONOMY BEFORE THE GOLDEN AGE

Humans have practiced astronomy since the very dawn of civilization. An understanding of the

One of Caliph al-Mamun's crown jewels was his renowned observatory. This facility was used by many of the great minds of the Muslim world, including Al-Khwarizmi, to study the heavens and improve upon existing astronomical scholarship.

progression of the sun enabled people to predict the seasons and judge when to plant and harvest crops. The prehistoric monument Stonehenge, for example, functioned as an observatory as early as 3000 BCE. The ancient Egyptians worshipped the stars, and they aligned the pyramids according to the positions of the stars.

The Babylonians were the first to develop an advanced form of astronomy. They recorded their observations and calculations on cuneiform tablets. As early as 1800 BCE, Babylonian astronomers began to develop a solar calendar that marked the phases of the moon. They were able to predict eclipses and chart

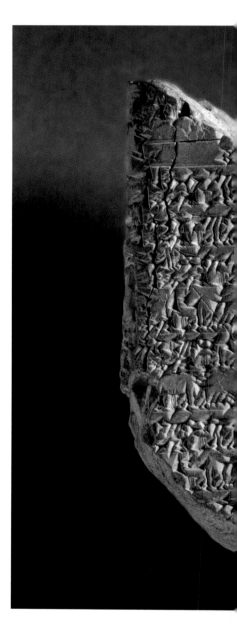

The Babylonians were early students of astronomy. This carved clay astronomical tablet records the rising and settings of Venus from the first six years of the reign of the king of Babylon, in the seventh century.

the courses of the planets Mercury, Venus, Mars, Jupiter, and Saturn.

Greek astronomers incorporated the discoveries of the Babylonians and greatly contributed to the theoretical knowledge of astronomy. One of the earliest Greek astronomers, Thales of Miletus, may have studied at a Babylonian school around 640 BCE. The Greeks often used the geometry of circles and spheres in their astronomy. Eudoxus of Cnidus was the first Greek astronomer to try to explain the movement of heavenly bodies. In about 370 BCE, he put forth the theory that the sun, moon, stars, and planets were affixed to a number of huge transparent spheres, one nested inside the next. They revolved in various ways with the motionless Earth at their center. Aristotle and Apollonius of Perga used this model of the cosmos as the basis for their astronomical work. Greek astronomers of the third and second century BCE worked on a catalog of star positions, methods for determining the magnitudes and relative distances of the sun and moon, and the means of measuring arc length.

The two greatest Greek astronomers were Hipparchus and Ptolemy. Hipparchus theorized that celestial bodies orbited around Earth following the paths of various circles. He measured the solar year

cogniti orbif cum hif que fe
bi unguntur a choroorapl

Ptolemy's astronomical treatise, known as the *Almagest*, was so groundbreaking that it served as the definitive astronomy text for more than one thousand years after his death. The *Almagest* was translated into Arabic at the House of Wisdom at the same time al-Khwarizmi was there.

with only a six-minute discrepancy, and cataloged the positions of more than one thousand stars. Ptolemy refined Hipparchus's work on the lunar cycle and devised an original theory of planetary motion. Ptolemy compiled Greek knowledge of astronomy as well as his own theories in a work called the *Almagest*. Ptolemy's *Almagest* was the defining work on astronomical theory until the sixteenth century.

Islamic scholars first translated the *Almagest* into Arabic in 800. Al-Hajjaj, one of al-Khwarizmi's colleagues at the House of Wisdom, completed a superior translation in 827–828. Islamic astronomers accepted Ptolemy's model of the heavens revolving around a stationary Earth. They did not attempt to improve the theories behind Greek astronomy. Instead, they refined the calculations and observational data of star charts and planetary motion.

ASTRONOMY IN THE ISLAMIC WORLD

The study of astronomy in the Islamic Empire began in 771, when an Indian traveler brought a work called *Sindhind* to Baghdad. According to al-Biruni, the *Sindhind* was a Sanskrit version of the

Brahmasiddhanta, which was written in 628 by the eminent Indian astronomer and mathematician Brahmagupta. Caliph al-Mansur ordered that the work be translated into Arabic. Mohammad al-Fazari, the first Islamic astronomer, completed the translation, titled *Zij al-Sindhind*, around 800. *Zij* means "set of astronomical tables."

Al-Khwarizmi's astronomical work, also titled *Zij al-Sindhind*, was a revision of the original version. He incorporated elements of Greek astronomy and also made his own original contributions. Over the course of his career, he worked on two editions of his *Zij*. There is no Arabic version of the work still in existence. Even so, it is the earliest Arabic language work on astronomy that still survives in anything like its original form.

Historians have been able to deduce much of the contents of al-Khwarizmi's *Zij*. Around 1000, the Spanish Islamic astronomer Maslama al-Majriti, who lived in Cordova, produced a revised version of the work. His student Ibn al-Saffar may have added further revisions. Adelard of Bath translated this version into Latin in the twelfth century.

Islamic astronomers who came after al-Khwarizmi wrote commentaries on his *Zij* and made references to it in their work. The astronomer al-Farghani produced a criticism of *Zij* in the second half of the ninth century. Al-Muthanna mentions al-Farghani's book in his own commentary on *Zij*, written in the tenth century. Neither work survives in Arabic, although al-Muthanna's commentary exists in Hebrew and Latin translations. In the introduction, al-Muthanna states that "the explanations in al-Farghani's treatise [lacked] completeness." It is possible that al-Muthanna's commentary is merely an expansion of al-Farghani's criticism. In any case, al-Muthanna presented his points in the form of questions and answers concerning al-Khwarizmi's *Zij* and gives a fair idea of the scope of the original work.

Al-Khwarizmi's *Zij* consisted of tables and instructions for calculating the positions of the sun, moon, and planets. Other tables addressed calculations for eclipses, visibility of the moon, and trigonometric functions. Al-Khwarizmi also discussed various calendars and methods for determining the time of day.

In his book *The History of Algebra*, B. L. van der Waerden quotes the historian Ibn al-Qifti on the sources al-Khwarizmi drew on for his *Zij*:

> He used in his tables the mean motions of the *Sindhind*, but he deviated from it in the equations (of the planets) and in the obliquity (of the ecliptic). He fixed the equations according to the method

of the Persians, and the declination of the sun according to the method of Ptolemy.

Ibn al-Qifti is saying, essentially, that al-Khwarizmi used Ptolemy's astronomy and the "method of the Persians" as well as the *Sindhind* in compiling the various tables. Al-Khwarizmi learned this "method of the Persians" from a Sassanid work, *Zij al-Shah*, written around 550.

INSTRUMENTS OF THE TRADE

If a modern student of science were to travel back to al-Mamun's observatory, it is likely that he or she would not immediately recognize the instruments or the purpose of the structure. Telescopes had not yet been invented. Astronomers used instruments such as astrolabes, quadrants, sundials, and celestial globes to observe the motion of the heavens.

Islamic astronomers made important advances in the development of these instruments. The astrolabe, the most important observational instrument of the time, was invented by the Greeks. Al-Fazari was the first Islamic astronomer to construct an astrolabe, probably in 777. Islamic scientists perfected the design of the astrolabe, and it was the primary instrument used for navigation until it was replaced by the quadrant in the eighteenth century.

The word "astrolabe" is derived from the Latin roots *astro*, for star, and *labio*, for finder. It consists of two plates. A solid plate called the tympan is engraved with lines representing the horizon, various altitudes, and other data for a certain latitude. It is overlaid with a rotating plate called the rete that has sections cut out so as to leave pointers representing the brightest stars in the sky. On the back is a movable sighting bar and an engraving of the circle of degrees of a circle. The astronomer measures the altitude of a certain star with the sighting bar, and then turns the rete on the

recording measurements. The seated figure in the center uses an astrolabe. The astronomers at al-Mamun's observatory made significant improvements to the astrolabe and other instruments.

other side of the astrolabe until the pointer for the star matches the corresponding altitude line on the tympan. By measuring the position of heavenly bodies, the astrolabe provided information for timekeeping, determination of geographical position, and astrological procedures.

Al-Khwarizmi wrote two works on the astrolabe, *Kitab 'Amal al-Asturlab*, or *Book on the Construction of the Astrolabe*, and *Kitab al-'Amal bi'l-Asturlab*, or *Book on the Operation of the Astrolabe*. Both have been lost. It is believed, however, that al-Farghani included al-Khwarizmi's *Book on the Operation of the Astrolabe* in one of his works. This section of al-Farghani's work explains how the astrolabe can be used to find the altitude of the sun, determine one's location, and solve various other astronomical problems.

Al-Khwarizmi also wrote a book called *Kitab al-rukhama*, or *On the Sundial*, which has also been lost. The precision of timekeeping devices such as the sundial was very important in the Islamic Empire for religious reasons. Muslims must offer prayers toward Mecca at five precise times every day. Islamic scientists used instruments and mathematical calculations in perfecting *ilm al-miqat*, the "science of the fixed moments" or timekeeping. The indicator bar of the sundial is set so that it is parallel to the axis of Earth. It casts a shadow that changes in length and angle throughout the day. The shadow also changes throughout the cycle of a year. Islamic astronomers calculated shadow length and the corresponding height of the sun and recorded them in tables, which were distributed across the empire.

The Islamic faith also necessitated a precise calendar, which was devised by astronomers. A new lunar calendar was established in the seventh century. It measures the years following the Hegira, or Muhammad's flight from Mecca. In the lunar calendar, the first appearance of the crescent moon marks the beginning of each month.

The study of calendars remained a subject of interest for Islamic astronomers. They were constantly looking for ways to revise the calendar to improve the accuracy of astronomical measurements. Al-Khwarizmi, for example, studied the Jewish calendar. He described it in a short treatise called *Istikhraj ta'Rikh al-Yahud*, or *About the Jewish Calendar*, one of al-Khwarizmi's few Arabic texts that still exists. It is a well-researched work that gives historians insight into the development of the Jewish calendar. The Jewish calendar is based on both the solar and lunar cycles.

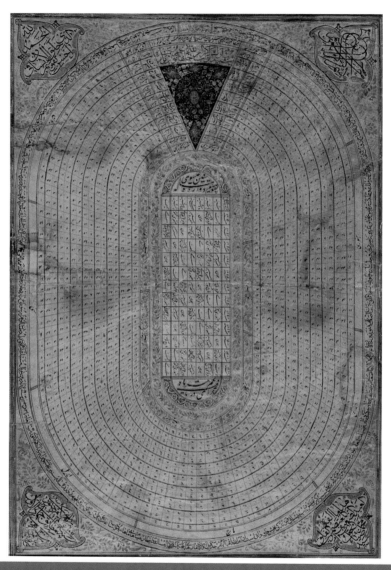

The Islamic calendar is a lunar calendar of 354 days divided into 12 months. This calendar begins in the year 622, when Muhammad and his followers immigrated to Medina. Muslim astronomers used their measurements and observations to devise the calendar.

In order to coordinate the two systems, a month is added to the year seven times during a nineteen-year cycle. The year begins with the month of Tishri, but a number of factors may delay the beginning of the month by a day. Al-Khwarizmi calculated the amount of time between the Jewish era—the time of the book of Genesis in the Bible—and the era of the Seleucid dynasty of the second and first century BCE. He also states the rules for calculating longitudes of the sun and moon according to the Jewish calendar.

Al-Khwarizmi's *Kitab al-Ta'rikh*, or *Chronicle*, was an astrological account of history rather than a purely astronomical work. It has been lost, but Islamic scholars cite it as a reference for certain historical events. The *Chronicle* attempted to prove that history fulfills the predictions made by astrology. It included the horoscopes of various public figures. According to the tenth-century literary historian al-Isfahani, al-Khwarizmi once calculated the precise hour of the prophet Muhammad's birth by analyzing the events of his lifetime through astrology. The *Chronicle* may have been the source for al-Isfahani's account.

THE SCIENCE OF ASTROLOGY

Astrology is the practice of predicting and analyzing events on Earth through interpretation of the position of the stars and other celestial bodies. Through the history of civilization, many cultures have independently established systems of astrology, some of which are still used today. The Indians, Chinese, Egyptians, Babylonians, Greeks, and Mayans all developed unique astrological practices. Islamic astrology, like Islamic mathematics and science, drew on many sources.

During the time of al-Khwarizmi, astrology was considered a precise science closely related to astronomy. Muslim astrologers frequently used the same instruments and mathematics as astronomers in charting the positions of heavenly bodies and calculating how their configuration at particular times might affect life on Earth. Many caliphs and government officials employed astrologers. They built observatories for charting the stars that were used by both astronomers and astrologers.

Astrology was popular with people of all classes throughout the Islamic Empire, but there were some who opposed the practice. Religious authorities argued that Islam centers around a submission to the will of God and, therefore, prohibits making predictions. Some astronomers, such as al-Biruni, expressed doubt that studying the stars could truly foretell events on Earth. Despite these objections, astrologers could always find work predicting the outcome of events or determining the best times to begin certain activities, whether waging battles or digging wells. Even skeptics such as al-Biruni contributed to the huge body of astrological texts produced between the ninth and fourteenth centuries.

AL-KHWARIZMI'S GEOGRAPHY

Islamic religious practices also spurred the advancement of geography and mapmaking. Muslims must pray in the direction of Mecca five times a day. In order to do so, they need to know their own precise geographic location in relation to Mecca.

During the reign of Caliph al-Mamun, al-Khwarizmi and sixty-nine other scholars executed "the form of the earth," the first Islamic map of the world and the heavens. He also wrote a book on geography called *Kitab Surat al-Ard*, one of his few works that survives in Arabic. Although it literally means *Book of the Form of the Earth*, most historians refer to it simply as al-Khwarizmi's *Geography*.

Geography mainly consists of lists of the latitudes and longitudes for more than twenty-four hundred locations. It is divided into six sections: cities, mountains, seas, islands, the central points of certain geographical regions, and rivers. Entries for each section are arranged into seven "climata" based on latitude, and locations within each "clima" are listed according to longitude. Al-Khwarizmi gives details of the size and shape of mountains, seas, and islands, and he lists towns and any points of interest on the rivers.

Ptolemy also wrote a work called *Geography*, his most famous work after the *Almagest*. It discusses the techniques of mapmaking and lists latitudes and longitudes of locations for a map of the world. Ptolemy's *Geography* contains many inaccuracies, but his principles of mapmaking were scientifically sound. The work remained influential until the Renaissance.

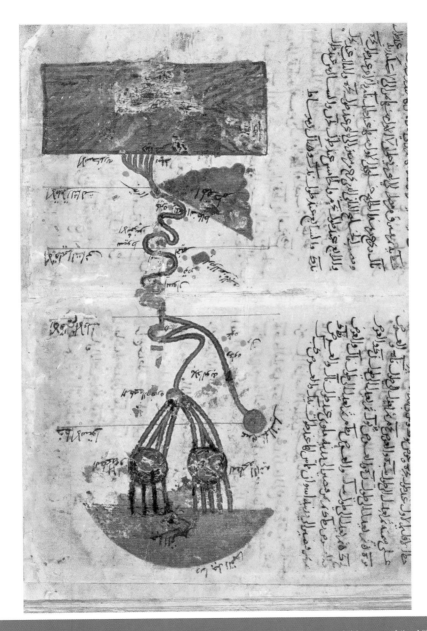

Al-Khwarizmi was also an accomplished geographer and mapmaker. He created this map of the Nile River from his exhaustive research, used in his book *Geography*. This work improved upon Ptolemy's earlier treatise of the same name.

Al-Khwarizmi consulted Ptolemy's *Geography* in writing his own. Al-Khwarizmi's work includes many of the same locations, some with identical latitudes and longitudes. But al-Khwarizmi's *Geography* is not a mere revision of Ptolemy's. The entries are organized according to a different system, and al-Khwarizmi's map differs significantly from Ptolemy's. It is generally more accurate than Ptolemy's map, especially in the regions of the Islamic Empire, Africa, and Asia.

THE LASTING INFLUENCE OF AL-KHWARIZMI

Al-Kwarizmi's contributions to science were important not only to the Islamic world, but to subsequent generations and other cultures. We can thank him for introducing us to the system of numbers we use today and for helping map Earth and charting the course of the universe's planets. And perhaps most significantly, al-Khwarizmi invented the study of algebra.

There is no doubt that al-Khwarizmi was one of the most influential mathematicians of the golden age of Islam. He lived at the ideal time for his work to be widely studied and appreciated. Caliph al-Mamun supported research and the translation of ancient texts, which helped lay a foundation for further achievements by Islamic scientists. Scholars who came after al-Khwarizmi recognized the caliber of the *Al-Jabr wa al-Muqabala*. They made copies that they passed on to other mathematicians and preserved in libraries and universities. Mathematicians such as al-Karaji and Omar Khayyam made further advancements in the study of algebra.

Historians acknowledge al-Khwarizmi's influence in mathematics, but they do not all agree that he was necessarily a great mathematician. There has been considerable speculation about the sources that al-Khwarizmi studied while writing his *Al-Jabr wa al-Muqabala*. Did al-Khwarizmi truly invent algebra, or did he merely compile and systemize the elements of algebra from the mathematic work of other cultures?

Al-Khwarizmi's successors in Islamic mathematics acknowledged him as the founder of the discipline of algebra. The tenth-century mathematician al-Kamil, for example, referred to al-Khwarizmi as "The one who was the first to succeed in a book of algebra and al-muqabala and who pioneered and invented all the principles in it," as quoted by Roshdi Rashed in *The Development of Arabic Mathematics*. Nevertheless, many historians have attempted to trace possible precursors to the mathematics in *Al-Jabr wa al-Muqabala*. Although many theories have been put forth, no historian has been able to conclusively prove al-Khwarizmi's debt to any single source.

Al-Khwarizmi's achievements are so vast and influential that the scholar was celebrated on a stamp in the former USSR in 1983 to commemorate the 1200th anniversary of his birth.

Several ancient cultures developed quadratic equations or other elements of algebra. Historians most often suggest that al-Khwarizmi may have used Greek, Hindu, Babylonian, or Hebrew sources.

In particular, scholars debate whether al-Khwarizmi was familiar with Euclid's *Elements* and whether it influenced his *Al-Jabr wa al-Muqabala*. Al-Hajjaj, the translator of Ptolemy's *Almagest*, also completed two different translations of the *Elements*, one under Harun al-Rashid and the other under al-Mamun. Al-Khwarizmi used geometric proofs for his equations, which indicates that he had studied some geometrical works. Al-Khwarizmi's style is very different from that of Euclid, though—he does not use formal axioms and definitions. The scholar Solomon Gandz, as quoted in B. L. van der Waerden's *History of Algebra*, hypothesizes that al-Khwarizmi purposely distances himself from Euclid's *Elements*.

Euclid and his geometry, though available in a good translation by his colleague, is entirely ignored by him when he writes on geometry. On the contrary, in the preface to his Algebra al-Khowarizmi distinctly emphasizes his purpose of writing a popular treatise that in contradiction to Greek theoretical mathematics, will serve the practical ends and needs of the people in their

affairs of inheritance and legacies, in their law
suits, in trade and commerce, in the surveying
of lands and in the digging of canals. Hence,
al-Khowarizmi appears to us not as a pupil of
the Greeks but, quite to the contrary, as the
antagonist of al-Hajjaj and the Greek school,
as the representative of the native popular
sciences.

Gandz puts forth an interesting theory, but this is only
his own interpretation of al-Khwarizmi's motives. There
is absolutely no evidence that al-Khwarizmi intentionally
neglected the Greek classics.

Al-Khwarizmi wrote about Hindu numerals and used
the Hindu *Sindhind* as the basis for *Zij*. Some Hindu influence can be identified in his *Al-Jabr wa al-Muqabala*.
In the second section, he uses a value of π and gives a
method for finding the circumference of a circle, which
may have been taken from Hindu sources. Hindu mathematicians were familiar with quadratic equations like
al-Khwarizmi's type. But al-Khwarizmi's presentation of
algebraic principles cannot be traced directly to any specific Hindu work.

Solomon Gandz put forth the theory that *Al-Jabr wa
al-Muqabala* borrowed material from an early Hebrew
treatise, *Mishnat ha-Middot*. Al-Khwarizmi's work on
the Jewish calendar shows that he was familiar with

"THE FIRST ENGLISH SCIENTIST"

Adelard (or Aethelard) of Bath was a twelfth-century scholar and philosopher who has been called the first English scientist. He studied and taught in France before leaving to spend many years traveling. He visited the famous medical school in Salerno, Italy, and proceeded on to Sicily. Arabs from North Africa had conquered the island in 965 and controlled it for about a century, and some Islamic influence remained. Adelard may have become fluent in Arabic in Sicily, or he may have learned the language while visiting Spain in his subsequent travels.

Adelard is known in particular for his study of Islamic philosophy and science. He translated a version of al-Khwarizmi's *Zij* into Latin, after which it was known as the Kharismian Tables. He also made two translations of Euclid's *Elements* from Arabic into Latin. One of the original Arabic versions is believed to have been al-Hajjaj's translation from Greek. He also translated works on astronomy and astrology. Paralleling al-Khwarizmi, Adelard wrote treatises on the astrolabe, cast horoscopes for members of the royal family, and advocated the use of Hindu numerals and the zero. Adelard is believed to have been the author of a mathematical treatise that, in part, discusses Indian methods of arithmetic. It has been speculated that it was based on al-Khwarizmi's work. Adelard was also a philosopher who promulgated the doctrine of indifference.

Like the scholars of the House of Wisdom of an earlier age, Adelard translated classic works and wrote his own. The circulation of these works contributed to a new age of learning.

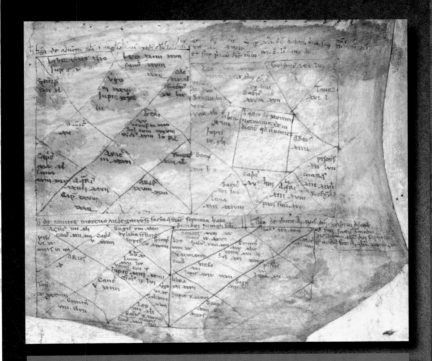

A set of royal horoscopes created by Adelard of Bath is in the British Library's permanent collection.

Jewish scholarship. Gandz, who studied the *Mishnat ha-Middot*, estimates that it was composed in the second century. Other scholars, however, believe that the work was actually written after al-Khwarizmi's time.

Gandz's discussion of al-Khwarizmi and his supposed rejection of Euclid's *Elements* do bring up al-Khwarizmi's goal of "writing a work that will serve the practical ends and needs of the people." Almost all of al-Khwarizmi's works were intended to serve a practical purpose. His *Geography* describes a map of the world. *Zij* provides tables and instructions for making astronomical calculations. The treatise on Hindu numerals systematically outlines the decimal number system and introduces the zero. Al-Khwarizmi's works on the astrolabe and sundial, perhaps written during the construction of al-Mamun's observatory, discuss practical aspects of observing the heavens. Even his *Chronicle* attempts to show that astrology is a rational branch of science. Unlike his colleague al-Kindi, al-Khwarizmi apparently never ventured into imprecise fields such as philosophy or religious thought.

Al-Khwarizmi's works were widely circulated after his death. His *Geography* remained influential in the Islamic world through the fourteenth century, although it was Ptolemy's *Geography* that most influenced

The work established by al-Khwarizmi and his colleagues at the House of Wisdom was studied by European scholars after the Dark Ages ended.

Western mapmakers. *Al-Jabr wa al-Muqabala* and a version of his treatise on Hindu numerals were eventually translated into Latin and greatly influenced Western mathematics. *Zij* was the first work of its type to be translated into Latin. Sections of the *Zij* were later included in the *Toledan Tables*, an assortment of astronomical tables drawn from the works of Islamic astronomers. This work was influential in Europe for more than a hundred years.

Although al-Khwarizmi's name is not familiar to the general public, his work is highly respected by historians and mathematicians. Although G. J. Toomer writes in *The Dictionary of Scientific Biography*, "Al-Khwarizmi's scientific achievements were at best mediocre," most experts hold al-Khwarizmi in much higher regard. In his monumental work *History of the Arabs*, Philip Hitti writes of al-Khwarizmi that, "One of the greatest scientific minds of Islam, he influenced mathematical thought to a greater extent than any other medieval writer." The renowned historian of science Roshdi Rashed rejects the idea that al-Khwarizmi's work was derived from older sources. He writes in *The Development of Arabic Mathematics* that "it is impossible to overstress the originality of al-Khwarizmi's algebra, which did not rise from any 'arithmetical' tradition."

Mohammad Khan highly praises al-Khwarizmi and his legacy to the Western world in his book *A Brief Survey of Muslim Contribution to Science and Culture* (as quoted by al-Daffa in *The Muslim Contribution to Mathematics*).

In the foremost rank of mathematicians of all times stands al-Khwarizmi. He composed the oldest works on arithmetic and algebra. They were the principal source of mathematical knowledge for centuries to come both in the East and the West.

In *The Universal History of Numbers*, Georges Ifrah sums up al-Khwarizmi's contributions to the modern world.

Unbeknown to him, al-Khwarizmi provided the name for a fundamental branch of modern mathematics, and gave his own name to the science of algorithms, the basis for one of the practical and theoretical activities of computing. What more can be said about this great scholar's influence?

622 The prophet Muhammad flees from Mecca to Medina, an event known as the Hegira.

632 The prophet Muhammad dies.
The caliphate is founded.

749 Baghdad is founded.

circa 780 Al-Khwarizmi is born.

786 Harun al-Rashid became the fifth caliph of the Abbasid dynasty.

813 Al-Mamun becomes caliph.

813–833 Al-Khwarizmi completes his *Al-Jabr wa al-Muqabala* and *Zij*.

833 Al-Mutasim becomes caliph.

836 Rebellion forces the caliph to move the capital to Samarra.

842 Al-Wathiq becomes caliph.

847 Al-Khwarizmi is present at al-Wathiq's death.
Al-Mutawakkil becomes caliph.

848 Al-Mutawakkil discontinues *mihna* begun by al-Mamun.

ca. 850 Al-Khwarizmi dies.

861 Al-Mutawakkil is assassinated.

892 The capital is restored to Baghdad.

1258 Mongols sack Baghdad and put an end to the Abbasid dynasty.

acrophonic Using a symbol to phonetically represent the initial sound of the name of an object.

algebra The branch of mathematics in which numbers and other elements of equations can be represented by letters.

astrolabe An instrument used to observe and calculate the positions of the sun and other celestial bodies.

astrology The practice of predicting and analyzing events on Earth through interpretation of the position of the stars and other celestial bodies.

axiom A statement that is accepted as truth without formal proof.

caliph The leader of a Muslim state, regarded as the successor of Muhammad.

cuneiform A script once used in Babylonia and other ancient societies.

geometry The branch of mathematics that examines points, lines, angles, surfaces, and solids.

hypotenuse The side of a right triangle that is opposite the right angle.

legacy Something passed on from an ancestor or predecessor.

observatory A building used for observing natural phenomena.

prophet In religious traditions, a knowledgeable person or teacher who conveys God's will to others.

Arab Science and Technology Foundation
P.O. Box 2668
Sharjah, United Arab Emirates
Website: http://www.astf.net
The Arab Science and Technology Foundation is an
        independent, nonprofit, nongovernmental
        organization that works regionally and
        internationally to encourage investment in science
        and technology.

The British Society for the History of Mathematics (BSHM)
20 Dunvegan Close,
Exeter, Devon EX4 4AF
England
Website: http://www.dcs.warwick.ac.uk/bshm/
        resources.html
The British Society for the History of Mathematics exists
        to promote and encourage research in the history
        of mathematics and the dissemination of the
        results of such research; to promote and develop
        for the public benefit, awareness, knowledge,
        study, and teaching of the history of mathematics;
        and to promote the use of the history of
        mathematics at all levels in mathematics
        education in order to enhance the teaching of
        mathematics for the public benefit.

Canadian Society for the History and Philosophy of
Mathematics
Rob Bradley, Dept. of Mathematics & Computer
Science
Adelphi University
Garden City, NY 11530
(516) 877-4496
Website: http://www.cshpm.org
The Canadian Society for the History and Philosophy of
Mathematics promotes research and teaching in
the history and philosophy of mathematics.

International Museum of Muslim Cultures
201 East Pascagoula Street
Jackson, MS 39201
(601) 960-0440
Website: http://www.muslimmuseum.org
The International Museum of Muslim Cultures is
dedicated to educating the American public about
Islamic history and culture, the contribution of
Muslims to the global community, and the
diversity of the Muslim community: past, present,
and future, including highlighting metropolitan
Jackson and the state's rich and diverse cultural
and religious heritage.

Islamic Educational, Scientific, and Cultural Organization
(ISESCO)
Avenue des F.A.R, Hay Ryad
P.O. Box 2275
PC Code 10104, Rabat
Kingdom of Morocco
Website: http://www.isesco.org.ma
ISESCO promotes cultural engagement and
coordination in education, science, culture, and
communication to highlight the achievements of
Islamic culture and support sociocultural
development. The organization works closely with
a number of international organizations on
dialogue projects, especially the United Nations.

The Islamic Information Centre
460 Stapleton Road, Eastville
Bristol BS5 6PA
England
Website: http://www.islamicinformationcentre.co.uk
The Islamic Information Centre is a source of Islamic
knowledge that offers a library of classical texts
that cover topics such as Tasfeer, Aqidah, Fiqh,
Tabaaqat (histories), and Hadith studies and
educates the non-Muslim public on the religion of
Islam.

Metropolitan Museum of Art
Islamic Art Division
1000 Fifth Avenue
New York, NY 10028
(212) 535-7710
Website: http://www.metmuseum.org/about-the-
museum/museum-departments/
curatorial-departments/islamic-art
The Metropolitan Museum of Art's collection of Islamic
art features nearly twelve thousand objects
ranging in date from the seventh to the nineteenth
century. Comprising sacred and secular objects,
the collection reveals the mutual influence of
artistic practices such as calligraphy and the
exchange of motifs such as vegetal ornament (the
arabesque) and geometric patterning in both
realms.

Museum of the History of Science
Broad Street, Oxford OX1 3AZ
England
Website: http://www.mhs.ox.ac.uk
The Museum of the History of Science houses an
unrivaled collection of early scientific instruments.
The museum offers a program of family-friendly
events, gallery tours, table talks, and education
sessions for schools.

Museum of Science and Technology in Islam
4700 King Abdullah University of Science & Technology
Thuwal 23955-6900
Kingdom of Saudi Arabia
Website: http://museum.kaust.edu.sa
This museum is part of King Abdullah University of
    Science and Technology. It explores Islamic
    contributions to science and technology.

WEBSITES

Because of the changing nature of Internet links, Rosen Publishing has developed an online list of websites related to the subject of this book. This site is updated regularly. Please use this link to access this list:

http://www.rosenlinks.com/PSMI/khwar

FOR FURTHER READING

Adamson, Peter, and Peter E. Pormann. *The Philosophical Works of Al-Kindi.* Oxford, England: Oxford University Press, 2012.

Al-Khalili, Jim. *The House of Wisdom: How Arabic Science Saved Ancient Knowledge and Gave Us the Renaissance.* New York, NY: Penguin Press, 2011.

Al-Khalili, Jim. *Pathfinders: The Golden Age of Arabic Science.* London, England: Penguin, 2012.

Belting, Hans. *Florence and Baghdad: Renaissance Art and Arab Science.* Cambridge, MA: Belknap Press of Harvard University Press, 2011.

Bobrick, Benson. *The Caliph's Splendor: Islam and the West in the Golden Age of Baghdad.* New York, NY: Simon & Schuster, 2012.

Flood, Raymond, and Robin J. Wilson. *Great Mathematicians.* New York, NY: Rosen Publishing, 2013.

Freely, John. *Light from the East: How the Science of Medieval Islam Helped to Shape the Western World.* New York, NY: Palgrave Macmillan, 2011.

Fuess, Albrecht, and Jan-Peter Hartung. *Court Cultures in the Muslim World: Seventh to Nineteenth Centuries.* New York, NY: Routledge, 2011.

Lapidus, Ira M. *A History of Islamic Societies.* New York, NY: Cambridge University Press, 2014.

Nardo, Don. *The Birth of Islam.* Greensboro, NC: Morgan Reynolds Publishing, 2012.

Rashed, Roshdi, and Michael H. Shank. *Classical Mathematics from al-Khwarizmi to Descartes.* London, England: Routledge, 2015.

Romanek, Trudee. *Science, Medicine, and Math in the Early Islamic World.* New York, NY: Crabtree Publishing Company, 2012.

Ruthven, Malise. *Islam: A Very Short Introduction.* New York, NY: Oxford University Press, 2012.

Saliba, George. *Islamic Science and the Making of the European Renaissance.* Cambridge, MA: MIT Press, 2011.

Scherer, Lauri S. *Islam.* Detroit, MI: Greenhaven Press, 2012.

al-Daffa, Ali Abdullah. *The Muslim Contribution to Mathematics*. Atlantic Highlands, NJ: Humanities Press, 1977.

Goldstein, Bernard R., ed. *Ibn al-Muthanna's Commentary on the Astronomical Tales of al-Khwarizmi*. New Haven, CT: Yale University Press, 1967.

Hill, Fred James, and Nicolas Awde. *A History of the Islamic World*. New York, NY: Hippocrene Books, Inc. 2003.

Hitti, Phillip. *History of the Arabs*. New York, NY: Palgrave Macmillan, 2002.

Hourani, Albert. *A History of the Arab Peoples*. Cambridge, MA: The Belknap Press of Harvard University Press, 1991.

Ifrah, Georges. *The Universal History of Numbers: From Prehistory to the Invention of the Computer*. New York, NY: John Wiley & Sons, Inc., 2000.

Lapidus, Ira M. *A History of Islamic Societies*. New York, NY: Cambridge University Press, 1988.

O'Connor, J. J., and E. F. Robertson. "Adelard of Bath." Fife, Scotland: University of Saint Andrews School of Mathematics and Statistics, November 1999 (http://www-groups.dcs.st-and.ac.uk/~history/Mathematicians/Adelard.html).

Rashed, Roshdi. *The Development of Arabic Mathematics: Between Arithmetic and Algebra*. Boston, MA: Kluwer Academic Publishers, 1994.

Saunders, J. J. *A History of Medieval Islam*. Boston, MA: Routledge and Kegan Paul, 1972.

Semaan, Khalil I., ed. *Islam and the Medieval West: Aspects of Intercultural Relations*. Albany, NY: State University of New York Press, 1980.

Spuler, Bertold. *The Age of the Caliphs: History of the Muslim World*. Princeton, NJ: Markus Wiener Publishers, 1995.

Toomer, Gerald J. "Al-Khwarizmi, Abu Ja'far Muhammad ibn Musa." Charles C. Gillispie, ed. *Dictionary of Scientific Biography*. New York, NY: Charles Scribner's Sons, 1970–1980. Volume vii, pp. 358–365.

Turner, Howard R. *Science in Medieval Islam*. Austin, TX: University of Texas Press, 1997.

van der Waerden, B. L. *The History of Algebra: From al-Khwarizmi to Emmy Noether*. New York, NY: Springer-Verlag, 1985.

ABOUT THE AUTHORS

Bridget Lim has taught history and religion at the high school level. Currently, she is pursuing a PhD in Islamic Studies.

Corona Brezina is an author and researcher.

PHOTO CREDITS